AVENGERS K
THE ADVENT OF ULTRON
#3

JIM ZUB
SCRIPT

D1470158

WOO BIN CHOI with **JAE SUNG LEE**
PENCILS

MIN JU LEE
INKS

JAE WOONG LEE
COLORS

VC's CORY PETIT
LETTERS

WOO BIN CHOI with **JAE SUNG LEE, MIN JU LEE** & **JAE WOONG LEE**
COVER ART

AVENGERS VS. ULTRON is adapted from AVENGERS ORIGINS: SCARLET WITCH & QUICKSILVER #1, AVENGERS ORIGINS: ANT-MAN & THE WASP #1, and AVENGERS (1963) #57. Adaptations written by SI YEON PARK and translated by JI EUN PARK

AVENGERS created by STAN LEE and JACK KIRBY

Original comics written by SEAN McKEEVER, ROBERTO AGUIRRE-SACASA, and ROY THOMAS; and illustrated by MIRCO PIERFEDERICI, STEPHANIE HANS, and JOHN BUSCEMA

Editor SARAH BRUNSTAD
Manager, Licensed Publishing JEFF REINGOLD
VP, Brand Management & Development, Asia C.B. CEBULSKI
VP, Production & Special Projects JEFF YOUNGQUIST
SVP Print, Sales & Marketing DAVID GABRIEL
Associate Manager, Digital Assets JOE HOCHSTEIN
Associate Managing Editor ALEX STARBUCK
Senior Editor, Special Projects JENNIFER GRÜNWALD
Editor, Special Projects MARK D. BEAZLEY
Book Designer ADAM DEL RE

Editor In Chief AXEL ALONSO
Chief Creative Officer JOE QUESADA
President DAN BUCKLEY
Executive Producer ALAN FINE

ABDO
Spotlight

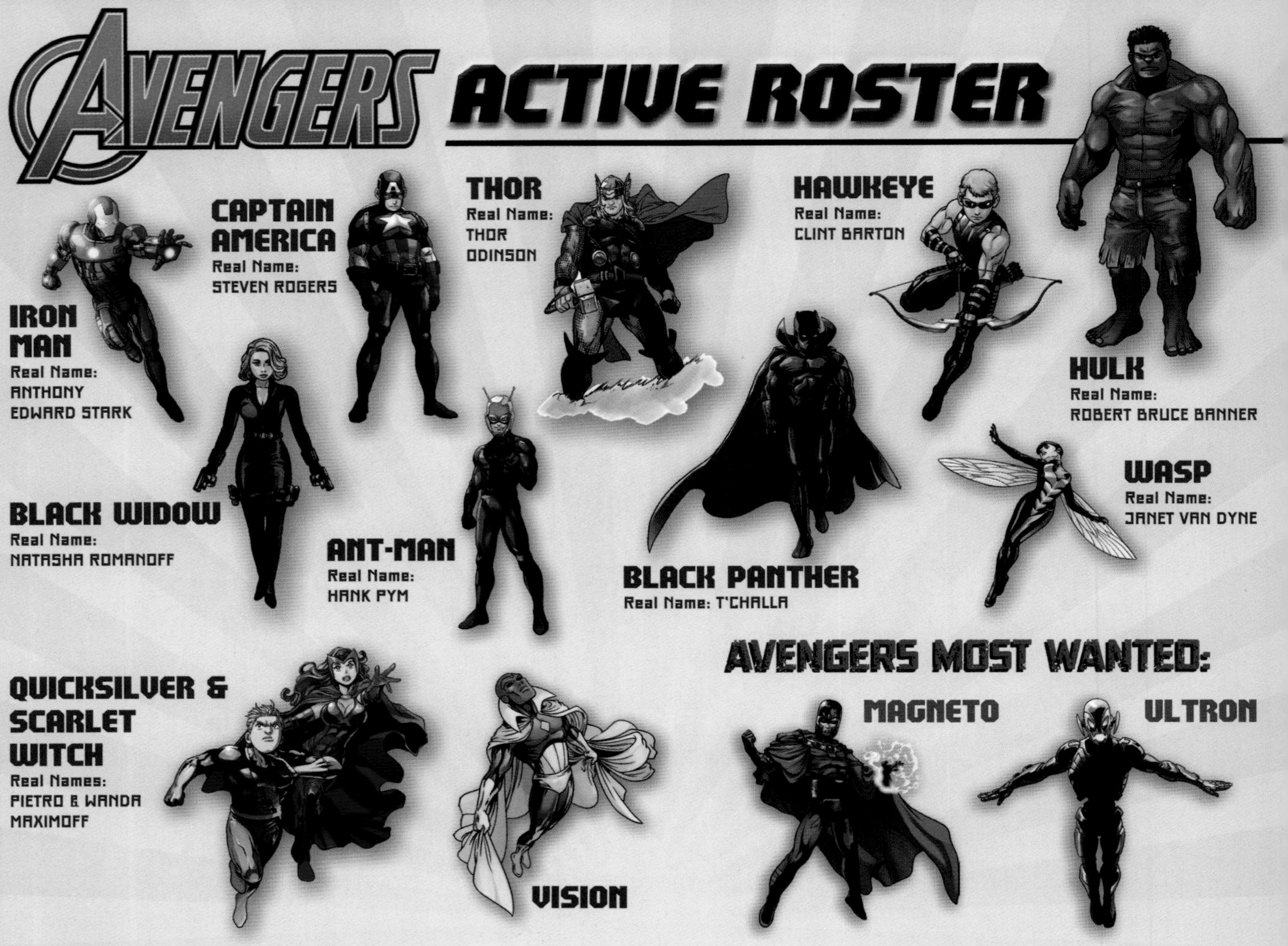
AVENGERS
ACTIVE ROSTER
IRON MAN
Real Name:
ANTHONY EDWARD STARK
CAPTAIN AMERICA
Real Name:
STEVEN ROGERS
THOR
Real Name:
THOR ODINSON
HAWKEYE
Real Name:
CLINT BARTON
HULK
Real Name:
ROBERT BRUCE BANNER
BLACK WIDOW
Real Name:
NATASHA ROMANOFF
ANT-MAN
Real Name:
HANK PYM
BLACK PANTHER
Real Name: T'CHALLA
WASP
Real Name:
JANET VAN DYNE
QUICKSILVER & SCARLET WITCH
Real Names:
PIETRO & WANDA MAXIMOFF
VISION
AVENGERS MOST WANTED:
MAGNETO
ULTRON

ABDOPUBLISHING.COM

Reinforced library bound edition published in 2018 by Spotlight, a division of ABDO, PO Box 398166, Minneapolis, Minnesota 55439.
Spotlight produces high-quality reinforced library bound editions for schools and libraries. Published by agreement with Marvel Characters, Inc.
Printed in the United States of America, North Mankato, Minnesota.
042017 092017

MARVEL
marvelkids.com

THIS BOOK CONTAINS RECYCLED MATERIALS

PUBLISHER'S CATALOGING IN PUBLICATION DATA

Names: Zub, Jim, author. | Choi, Woo Bin ; Lee, Jae Sung ; Lee, Min Ju ; Lee, Jae Woong, illustrators.
Title: The advent of Ultron / writer: Jim Zub ; art: Woo Bin Choi ; Jae Sung Lee ; Min Ju Lee ; Jae Woong Lee.
Description: Reinforced library bound edition. | Minneapolis, Minnesota : Spotlight, 2018. | Series: Avengers K Set 2
Summary: Learn about the beginnings of your favorite Avengers, including Quicksilver and the Scarlet Witch's time with Magneto, how Ant-Man and the Wasp became a team, and the Vision's struggle to understand where he came from.
Identifiers: LCCN 2016961923 | ISBN 9781532140013 (v.1 ; lib. bdg.) | ISBN 9781532140020 (v.2 ; lib. bdg.) | ISBN 9781532140037 (v.3 ; lib. bdg.) | ISBN 9781532140044 (v.4 ; lib. bdg.) | ISBN 9781532140051 (v.5 ; lib. bdg.) | ISBN 9781532140068 (v.6 ; lib. bdg.)
Subjects: LCSH: Avengers (Fictitious characters)--Juvenile fiction. | Adventure and adventurers--Juvenile fiction. | Comic books, strips, etc.--Juvenile fiction. | Graphic novels--Juvenile fiction.
Classification: DDC 741.5--dc23
LC record available at https://lccn.loc.gov/2016961923

ABDO
Spotlight

A Division of ABDO
abdopublishing.com

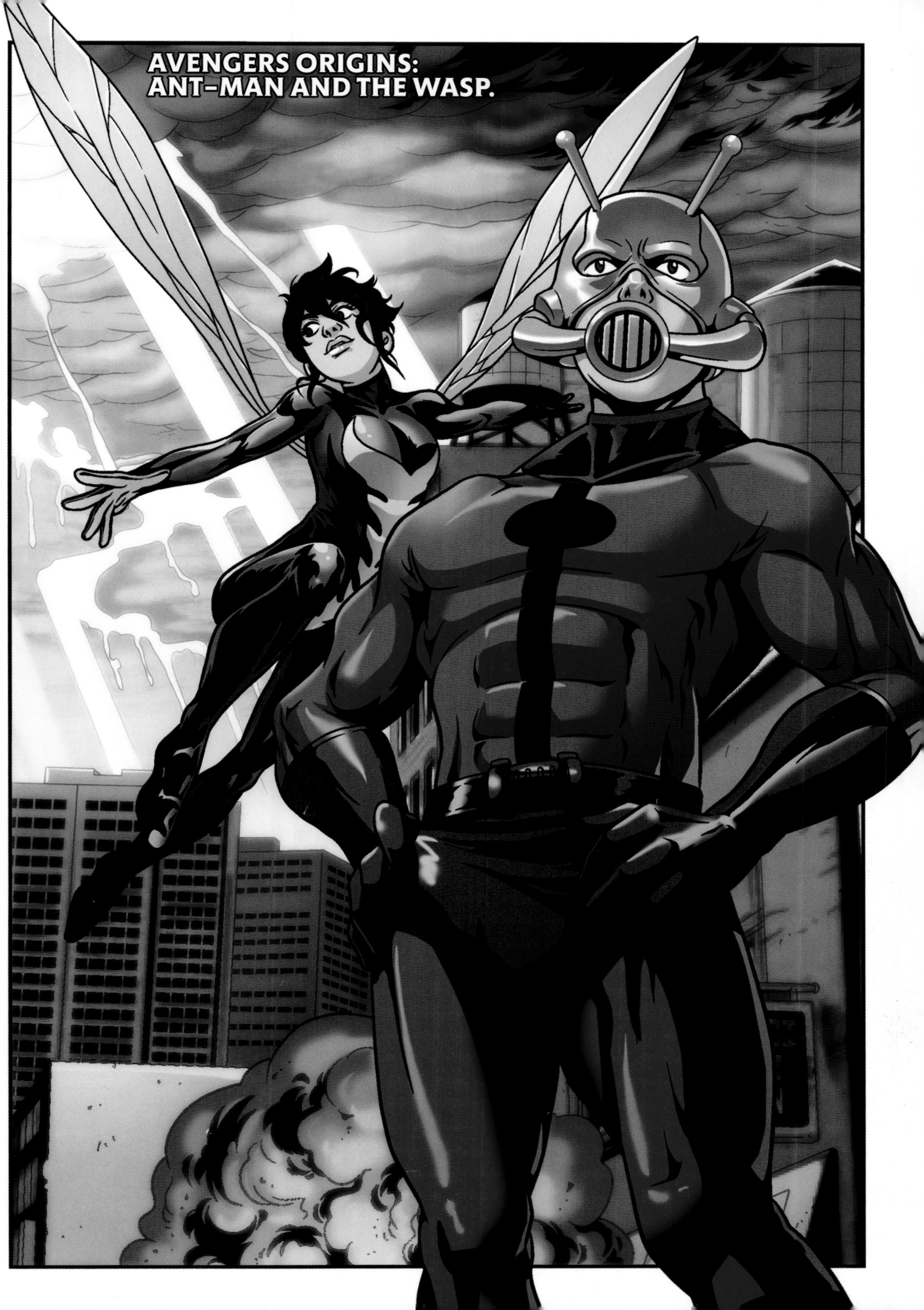
AVENGERS ORIGINS:
ANT-MAN AND THE WASP.

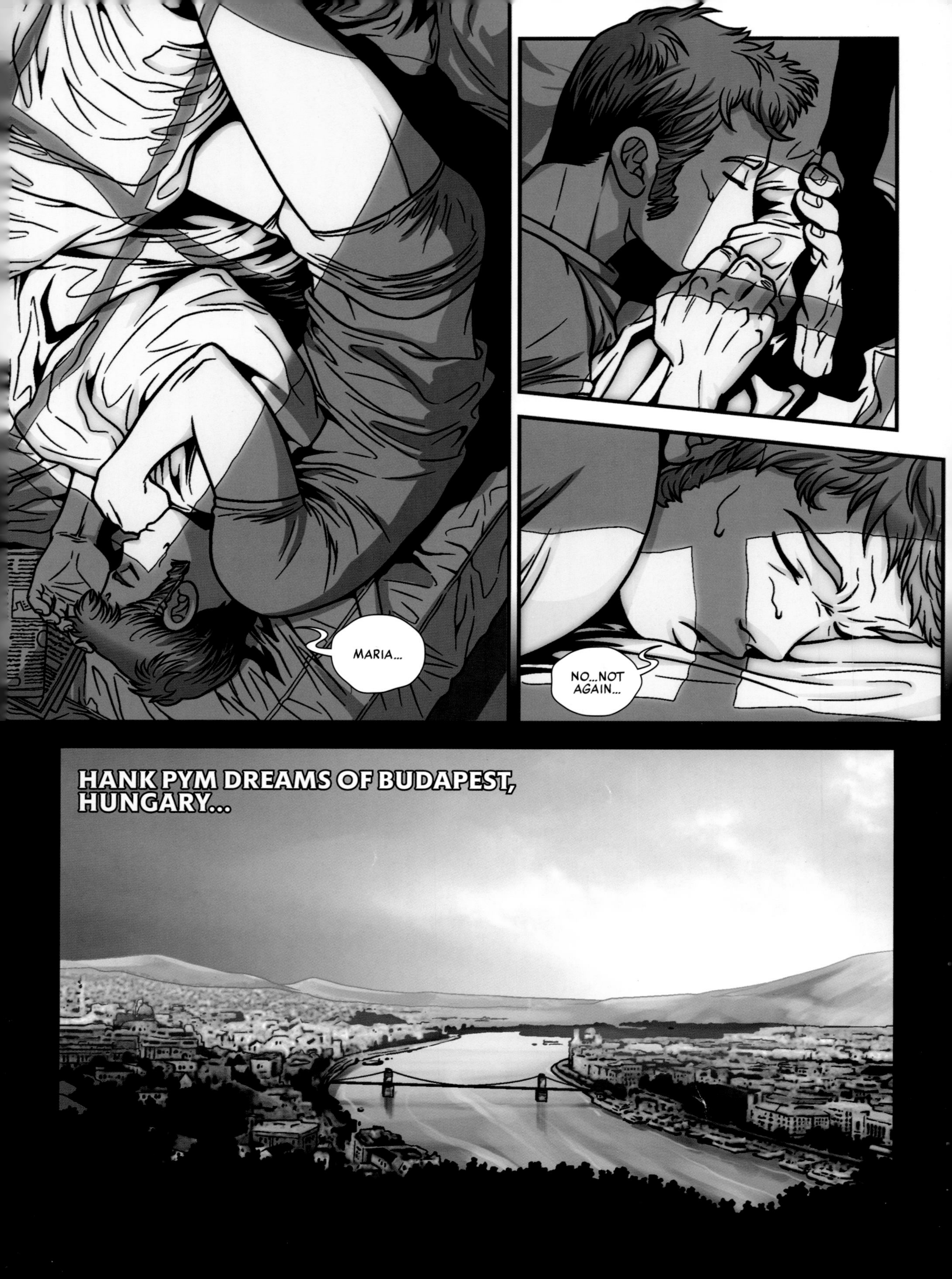
MARIA...
NO...NOT AGAIN...
HANK PYM DREAMS OF BUDAPEST, HUNGARY...

OH, HANK. I'M STILL WORRIED WE MADE A MISTAKE IN COMING HERE FOR OUR HONEYMOON.

I WANTED TO SEE WHERE YOU GREW UP, MARIA.

THE POLITICAL ENEMIES WE MADE, MY FATHER AND I...

...THEY HAVE LONG MEMORIES, AND THEY DON'T FORGIVE.

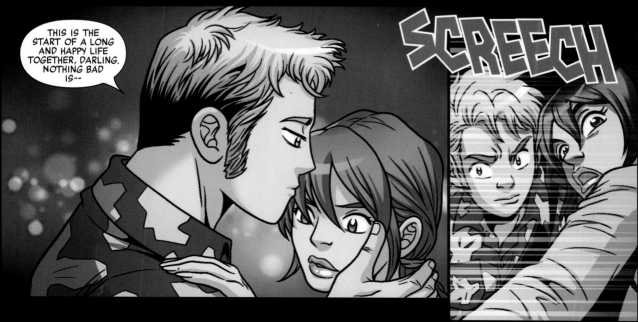

THIS IS THE START OF A LONG AND HAPPY LIFE TOGETHER, DARLING. NOTHING BAD IS--

SCREECH

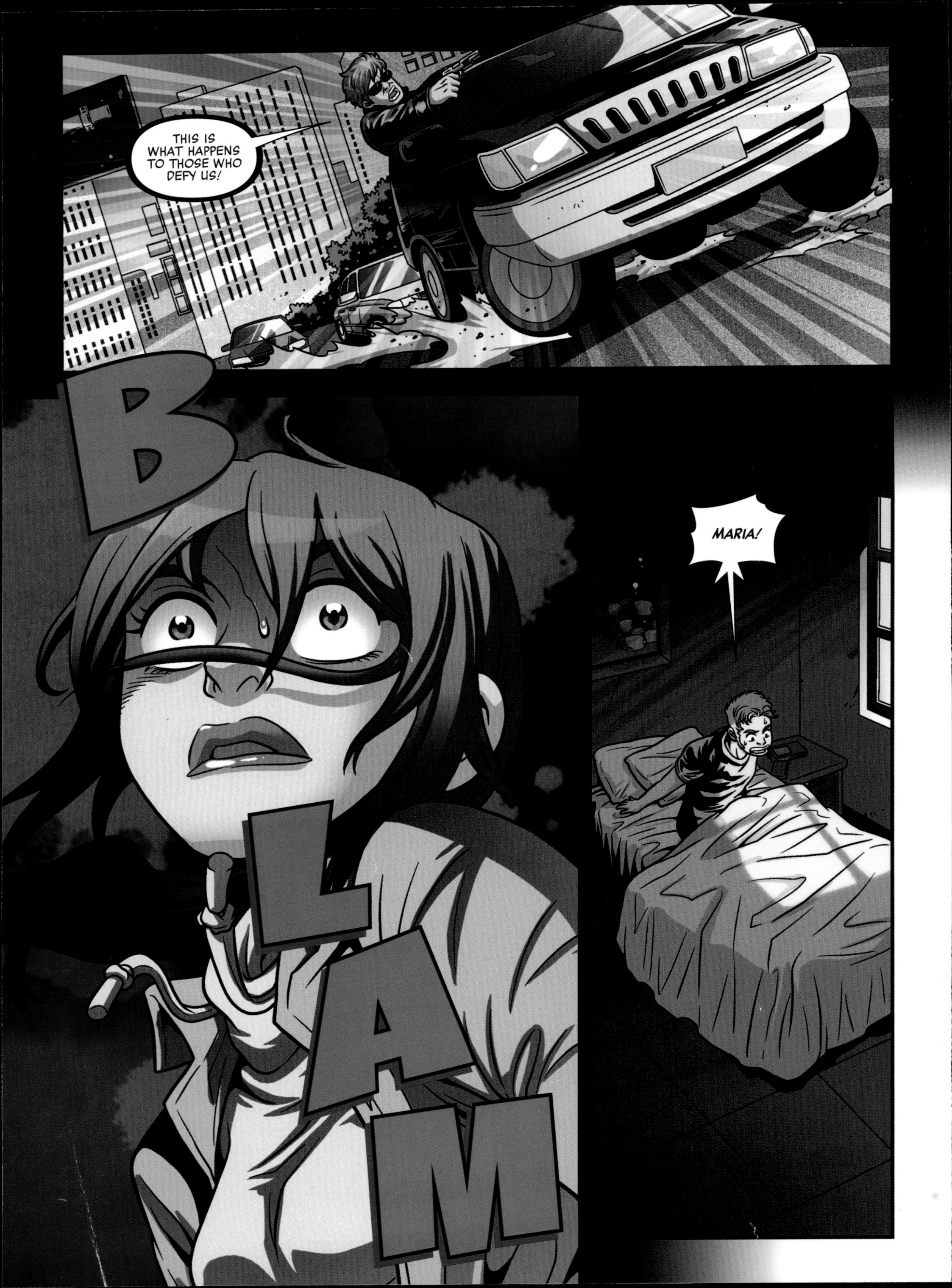
THIS IS WHAT HAPPENS TO THOSE WHO DEFY US!
BLAM
MARIA!

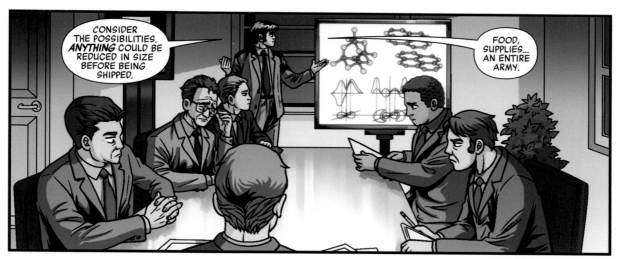

CONSIDER THE POSSIBILITIES. *ANYTHING* COULD BE REDUCED IN SIZE BEFORE BEING SHIPPED.

FOOD, SUPPLIES... AN ENTIRE ARMY.

AN *ARMY?*

ARE YOU DEVELOPING A WEAPON OF *WAR*, DR. PYM?

WHAT? NO, THAT WAS JUST AN EXAMPLE...

THIS IS A *HUMANITARIAN* FOUNDATION. WE DON'T FUND *WEAPONS* RESEARCH.

I DIDN'T MEAN IT LIKE THAT...

HAVE YOU EVEN TESTED THIS YET? ALL I SEE HERE IS A THEORY.

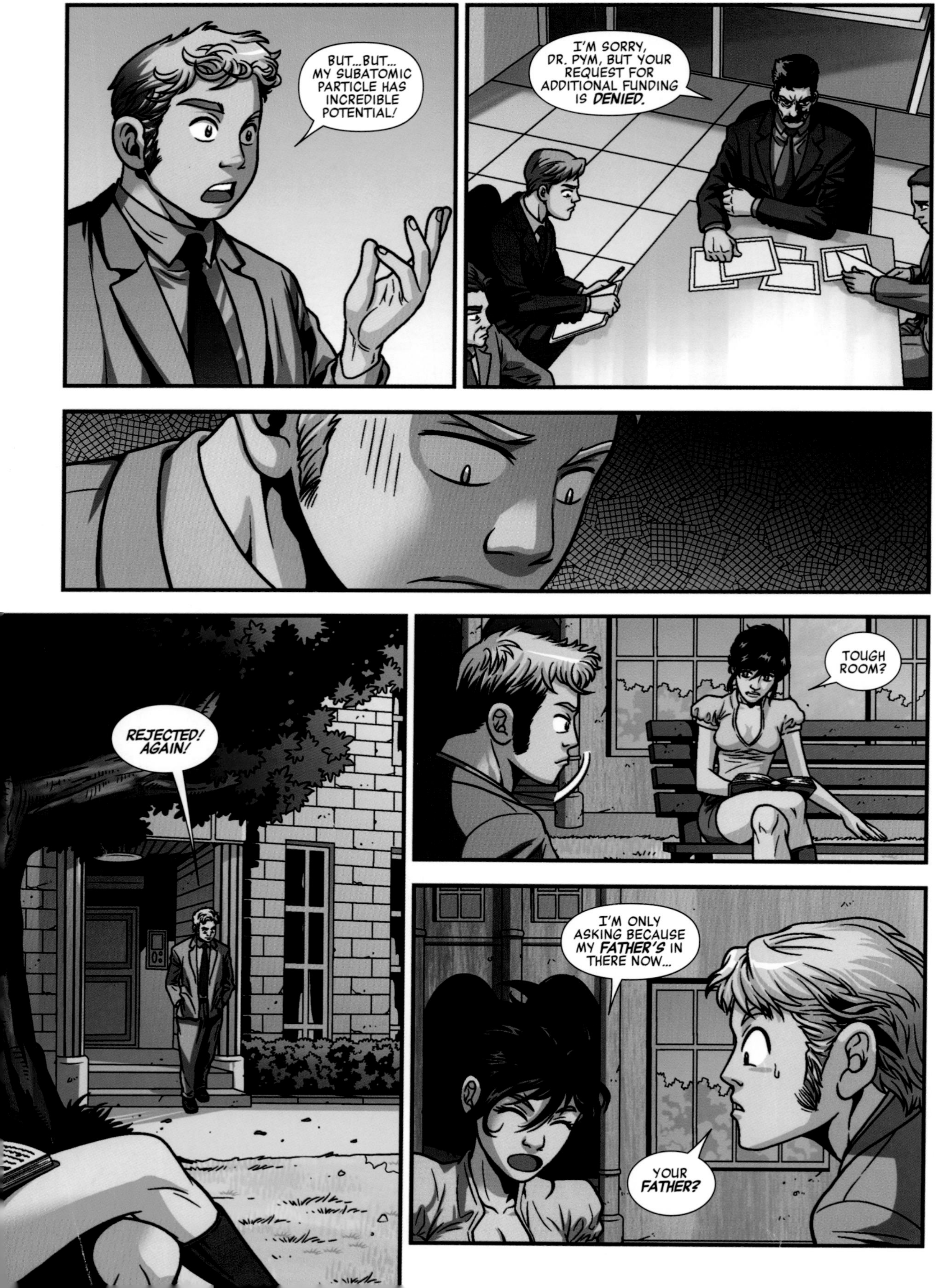
BUT...BUT... MY SUBATOMIC PARTICLE HAS INCREDIBLE POTENTIAL!
I'M SORRY, DR. PYM, BUT YOUR REQUEST FOR ADDITIONAL FUNDING IS DENIED.
REJECTED! AGAIN!
TOUGH ROOM?
I'M ONLY ASKING BECAUSE MY FATHER'S IN THERE NOW...
YOUR FATHER?

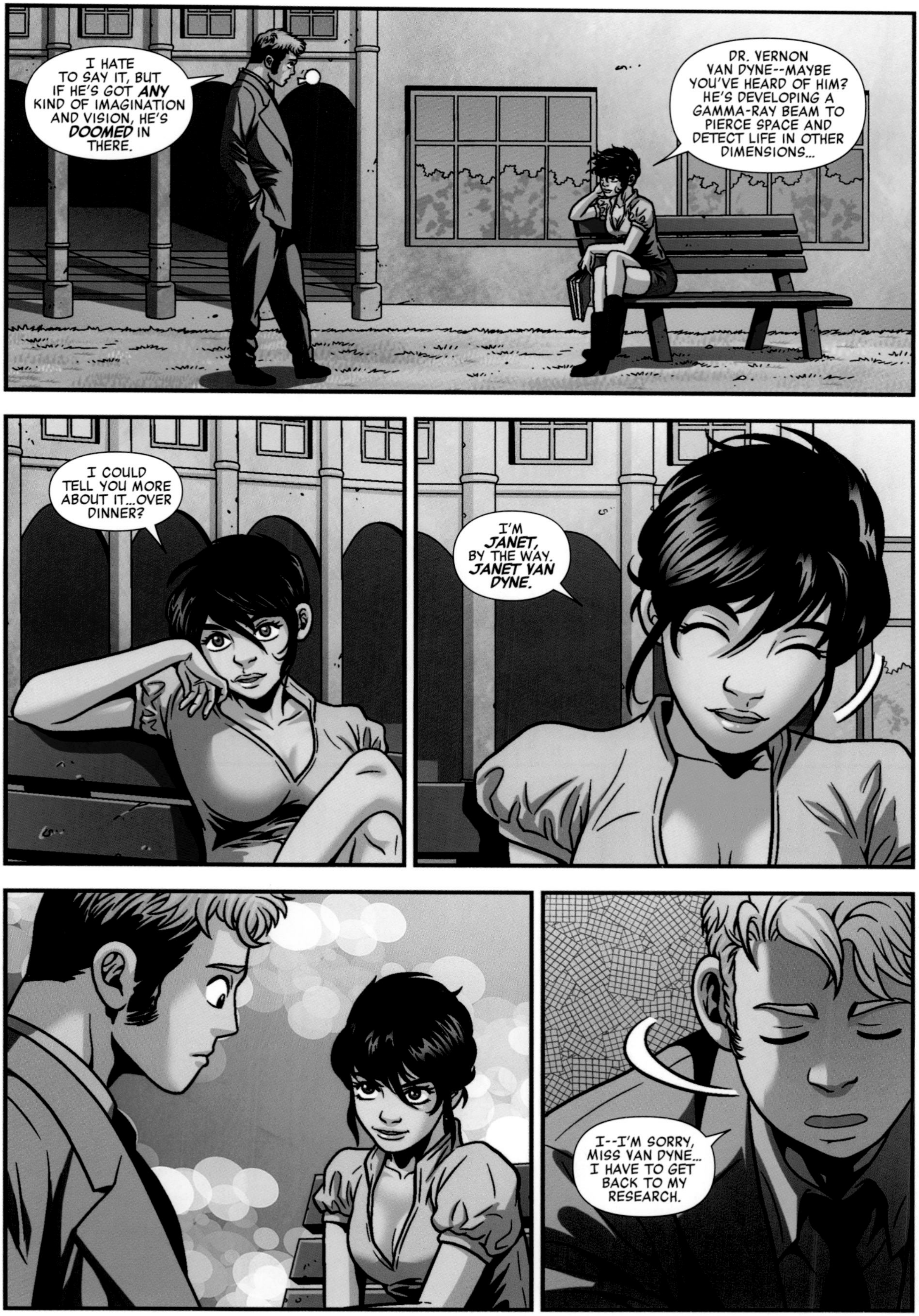
I HATE TO SAY IT, BUT IF HE'S GOT ANY KIND OF IMAGINATION AND VISION, HE'S DOOMED IN THERE.
DR. VERNON VAN DYNE--MAYBE YOU'VE HEARD OF HIM? HE'S DEVELOPING A GAMMA-RAY BEAM TO PIERCE SPACE AND DETECT LIFE IN OTHER DIMENSIONS...
I COULD TELL YOU MORE ABOUT IT...OVER DINNER?
I'M JANET, BY THE WAY. JANET VAN DYNE.
I--I'M SORRY, MISS VAN DYNE... I HAVE TO GET BACK TO MY RESEARCH.

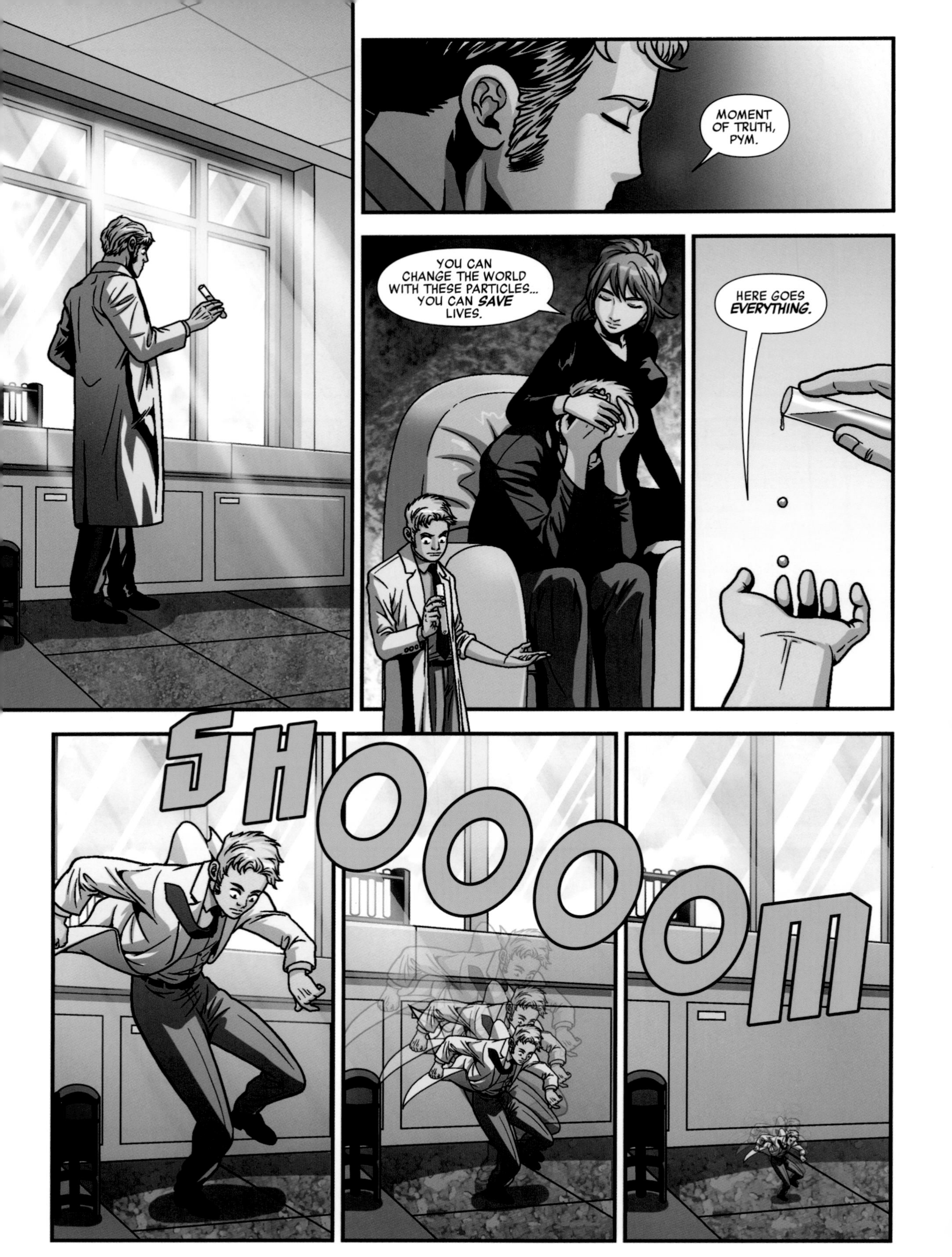
MOMENT OF TRUTH, PYM.
YOU CAN CHANGE THE WORLD WITH THESE PARTICLES... YOU CAN SAVE LIVES.
HERE GOES EVERYTHING.
SHOOOOOM

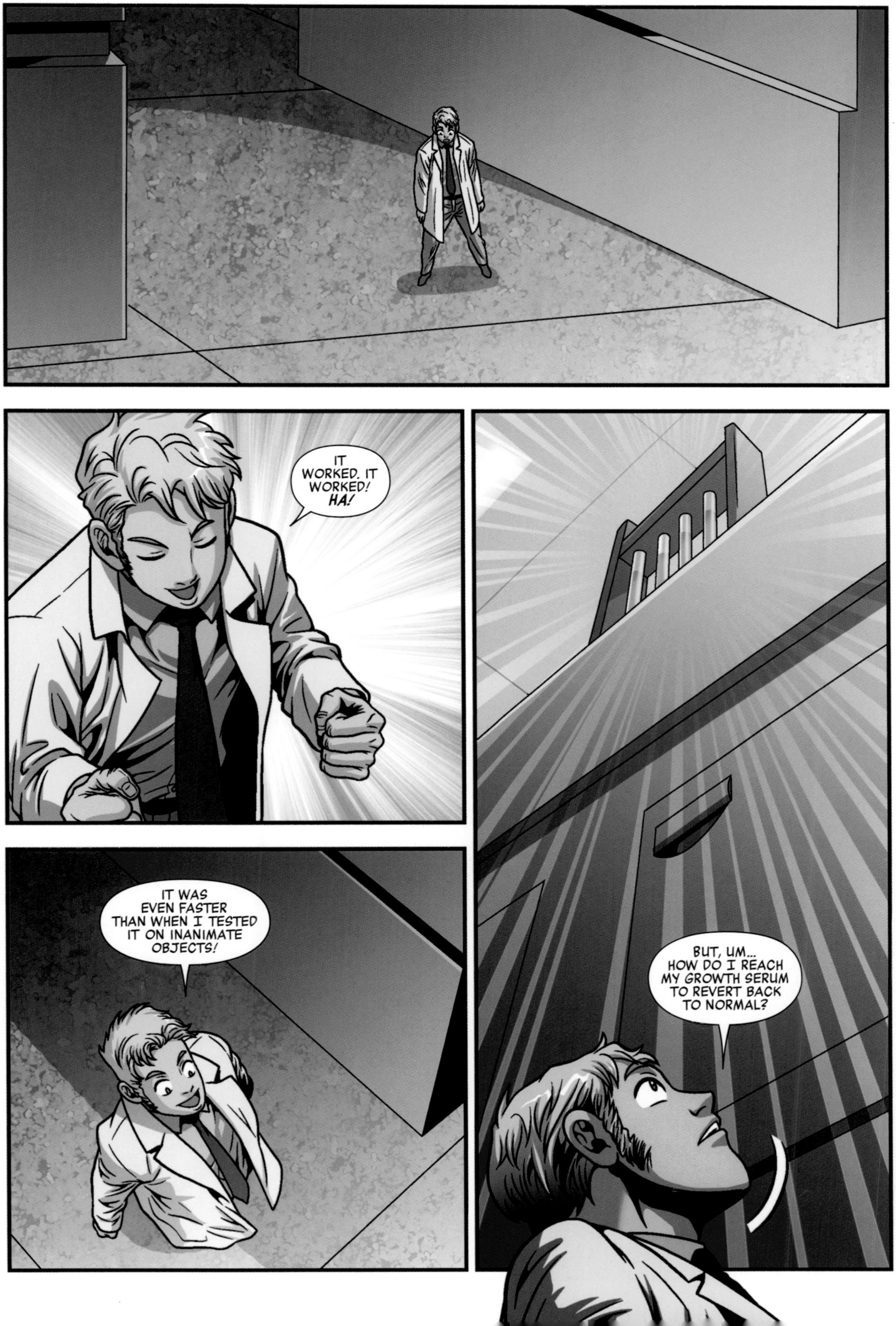
IT WORKED. IT WORKED! HA!
IT WAS EVEN FASTER THAN WHEN I TESTED IT ON INANIMATE OBJECTS!
BUT, UM... HOW DO I REACH MY GROWTH SERUM TO REVERT BACK TO NORMAL?

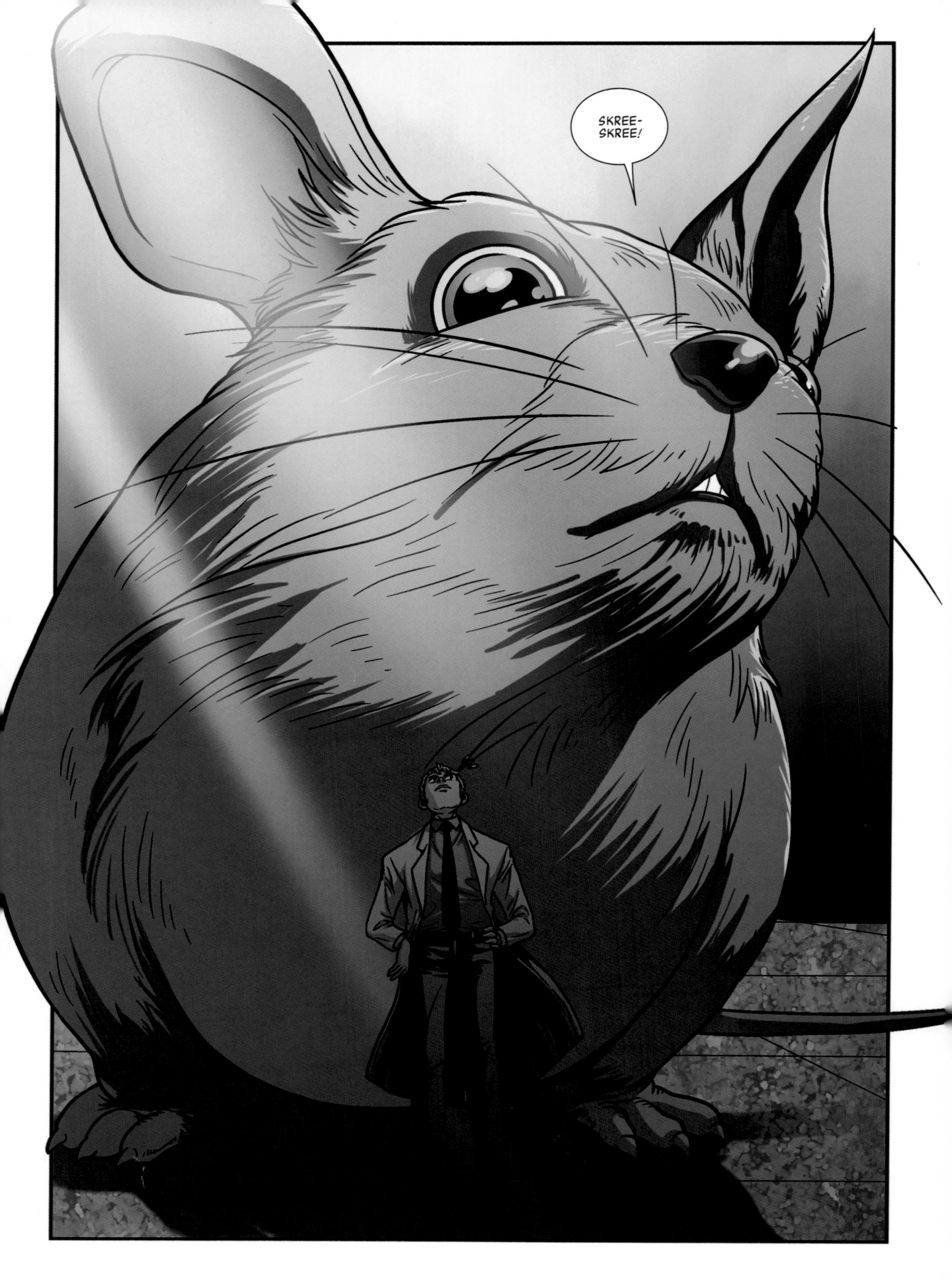
SKREE-
SKREE!

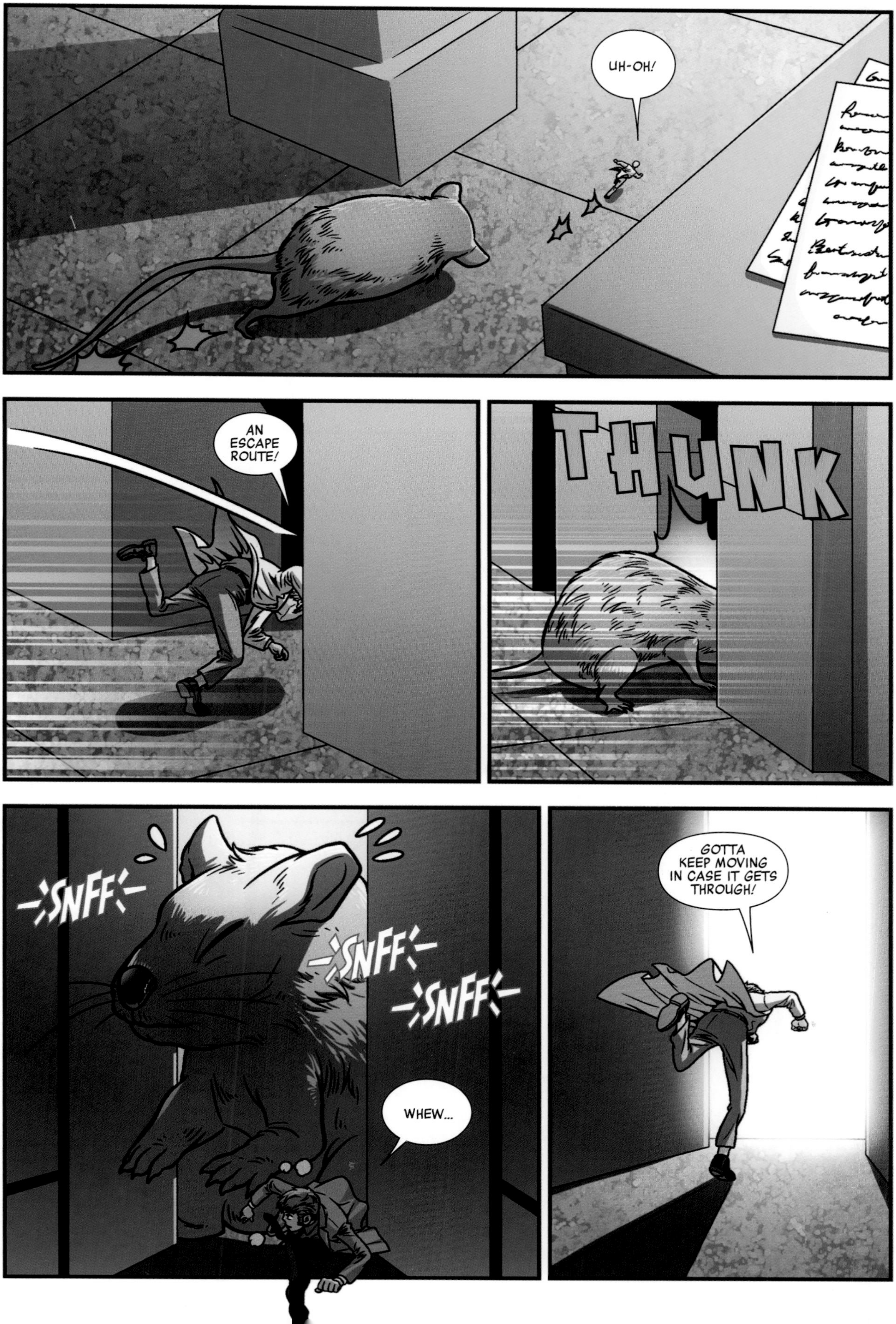
UH-OH!
AN ESCAPE ROUTE!
THUNK
SNFF
SNFF
SNFF
WHEW...
GOTTA KEEP MOVING IN CASE IT GETS THROUGH!

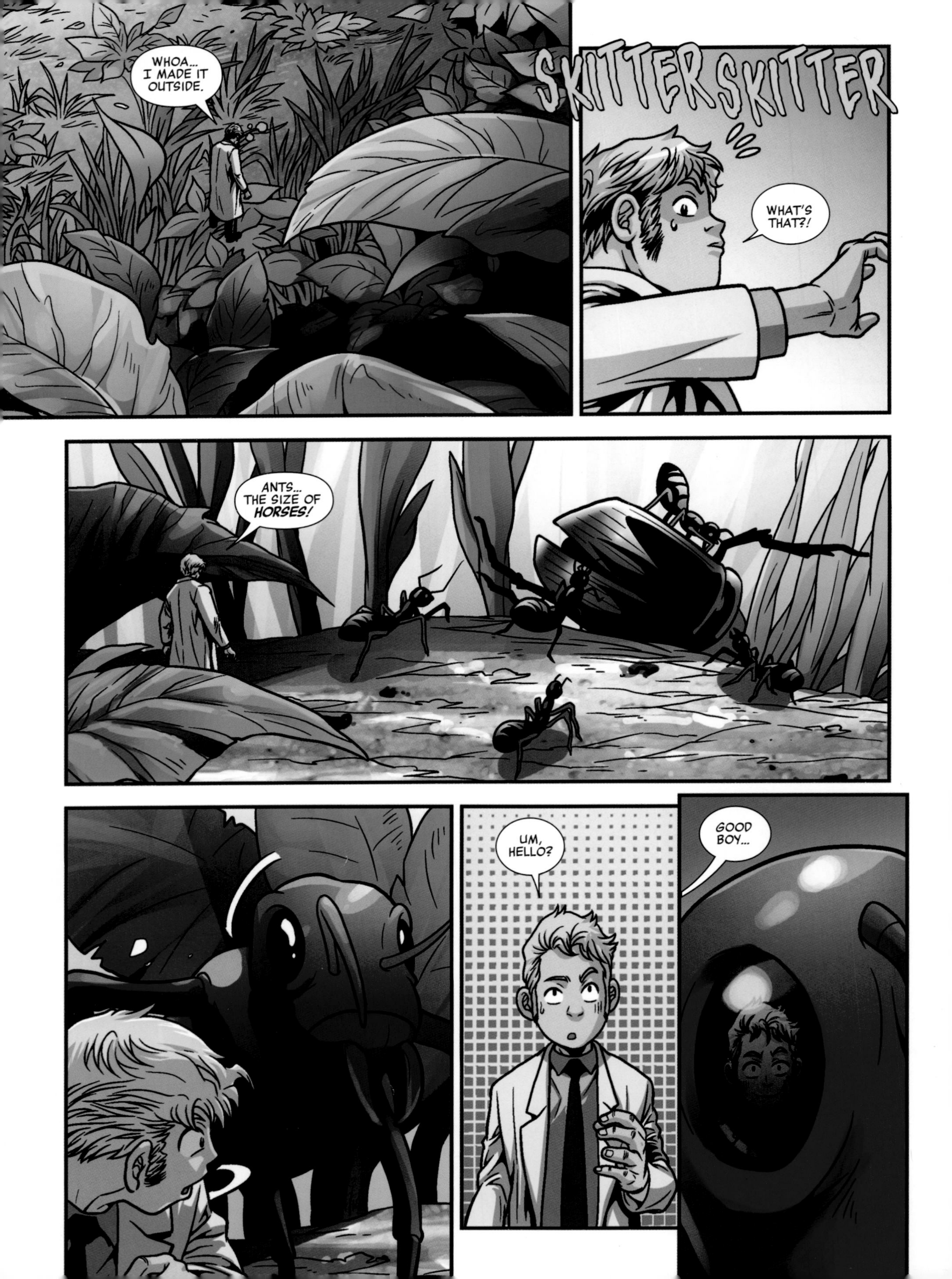
WHOA... I MADE IT OUTSIDE.
SKITTER SKITTER
WHAT'S THAT?!
ANTS... THE SIZE OF *HORSES!*
UM, HELLO?
GOOD BOY...

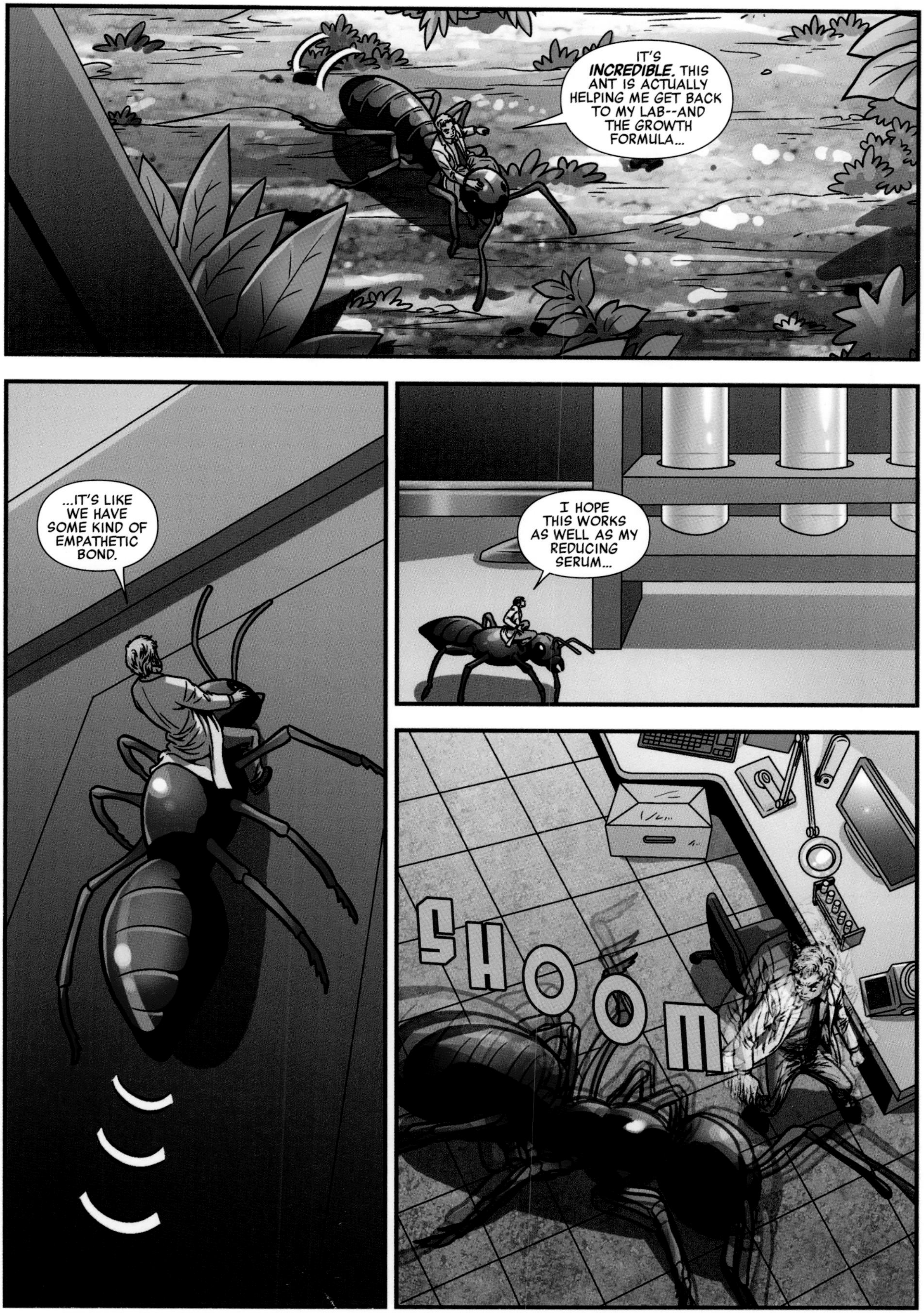
IT'S *INCREDIBLE.* THIS ANT IS ACTUALLY HELPING ME GET BACK TO MY LAB--AND THE GROWTH FORMULA...
...IT'S LIKE WE HAVE SOME KIND OF EMPATHETIC BOND.
I HOPE THIS WORKS AS WELL AS MY REDUCING SERUM...
SHOOM

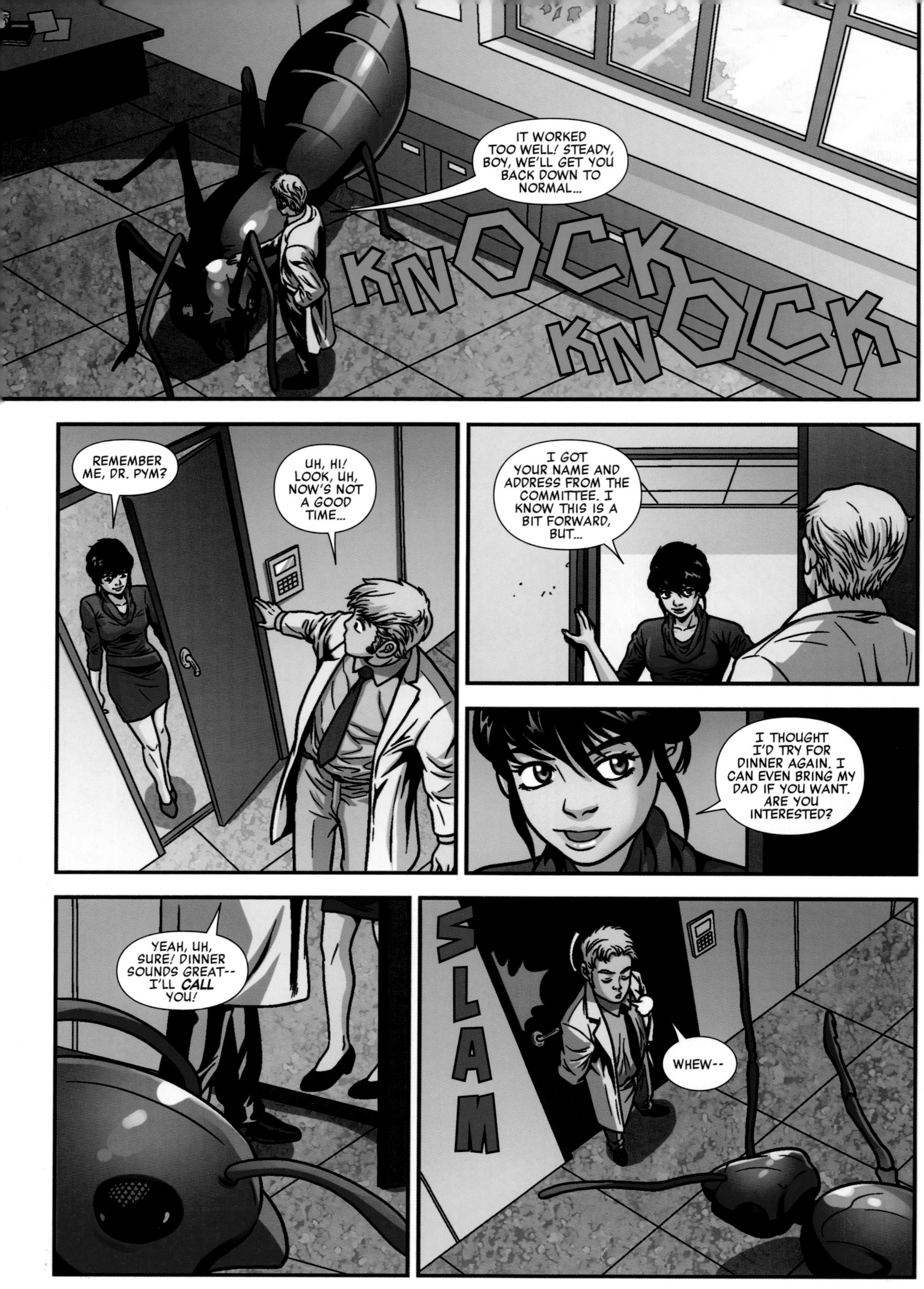
IT WORKED TOO WELL! STEADY, BOY, WE'LL GET YOU BACK DOWN TO NORMAL...
KNOCK KNOCK
REMEMBER ME, DR. PYM?
UH, HI! LOOK, UH, NOW'S NOT A GOOD TIME...
I GOT YOUR NAME AND ADDRESS FROM THE COMMITTEE. I KNOW THIS IS A BIT FORWARD, BUT...
I THOUGHT I'D TRY FOR DINNER AGAIN. I CAN EVEN BRING MY DAD IF YOU WANT. ARE YOU INTERESTED?
YEAH, UH, SURE! DINNER SOUNDS GREAT-- I'LL CALL YOU!
SLAM
WHEW--

UP UNTIL THIS POINT, I'VE SPECIALIZED IN MOLECULAR CELL TRANSITIONS.

WHEN YOU SAY "UP UNTIL THIS POINT," DOES THAT MEAN YOU'RE BRANCHING OUT?

DAD. *SERIOUSLY.* YOU PROMISED.

POSSIBLY, DR. VAN DYNE. JUST THIS AFTERNOON I BEGAN TO CONTEMPLATE A RADICAL *SHIFT* IN MY FOCUS.

ALL RIGHT, *FELLAS.* ENOUGH SHOP TALK.

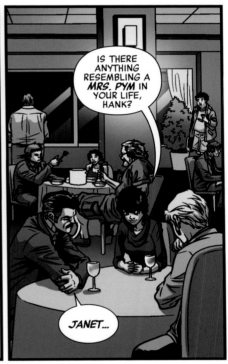

IS THERE ANYTHING RESEMBLING A *MRS. PYM* IN YOUR LIFE, HANK?

JANET...

I...THAT IS... THE NEW DIRECTION I'M CONTEMPLATING IS...*ENTOMOLOGY.* MORE SPECIFICALLY, HOW INSECTS COMMUNICATE...

HMMM...

ENTOMOLOGY, HUH? I LIKE BUGS...

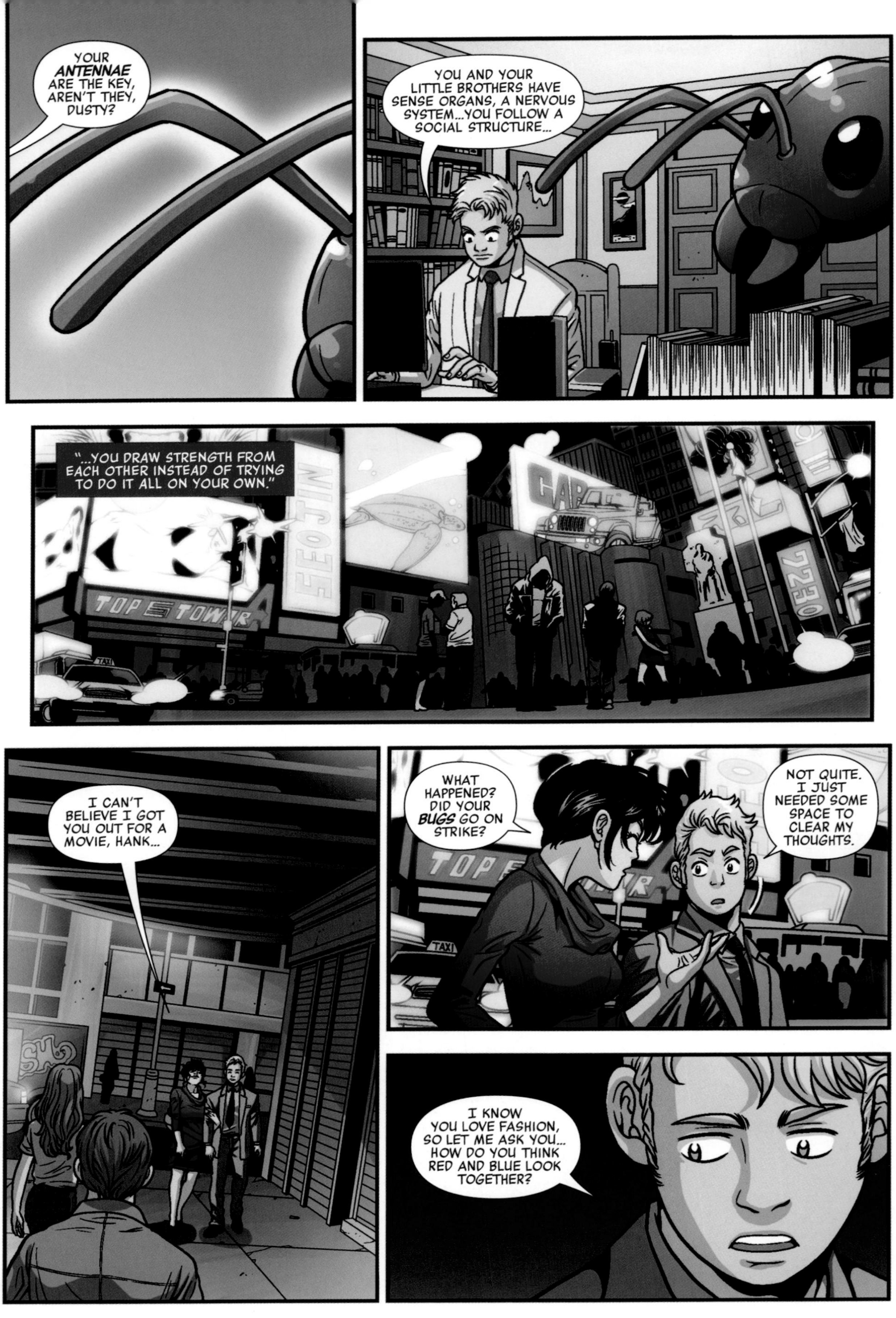
YOUR ANTENNAE ARE THE KEY, AREN'T THEY, DUSTY?
YOU AND YOUR LITTLE BROTHERS HAVE SENSE ORGANS, A NERVOUS SYSTEM...YOU FOLLOW A SOCIAL STRUCTURE...
"...YOU DRAW STRENGTH FROM EACH OTHER INSTEAD OF TRYING TO DO IT ALL ON YOUR OWN."
TOP TOWER
TAXI
I CAN'T BELIEVE I GOT YOU OUT FOR A MOVIE, HANK...
WHAT HAPPENED? DID YOUR BUGS GO ON STRIKE?
NOT QUITE. I JUST NEEDED SOME SPACE TO CLEAR MY THOUGHTS.
I KNOW YOU LOVE FASHION, SO LET ME ASK YOU... HOW DO YOU THINK RED AND BLUE LOOK TOGETHER?

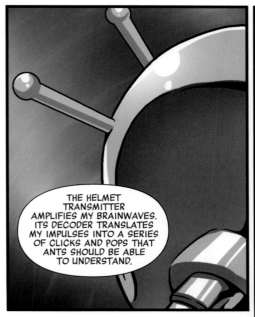

THE COSTUME PROTECTS ME FROM ANY RANDOM BUG BITES WHEN I SHRINK DOWN...AND IT LOOKS PRETTY COOL, TOO.

THE HELMET TRANSMITTER AMPLIFIES MY BRAINWAVES. ITS DECODER TRANSLATES MY IMPULSES INTO A SERIES OF CLICKS AND POPS THAT ANTS SHOULD BE ABLE TO UNDERSTAND.

THE RECEIVER ALLOWS ME TO "HEAR" RECIPROCAL EMISSIONS COMING FROM THEM.

OKAY, HERE GOES. INTO THE RABBIT HOLE AGAIN... ER, MAKE THAT ANT HOLE.

IT'S **WORKING!** MY HELMET IS REGISTERING THE ELECTRIC IMPULSES THE ANTS ARE EMITTING...

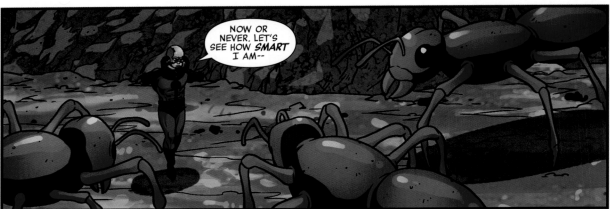

NOW OR NEVER. LET'S SEE HOW **SMART** I AM--

GOTTA FIND THE CORRECT WAVELENGTH... HURRY, PYM, HURRY!

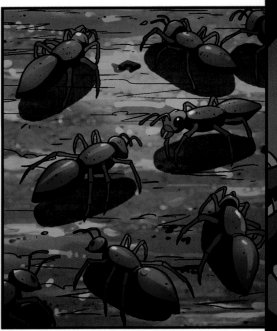

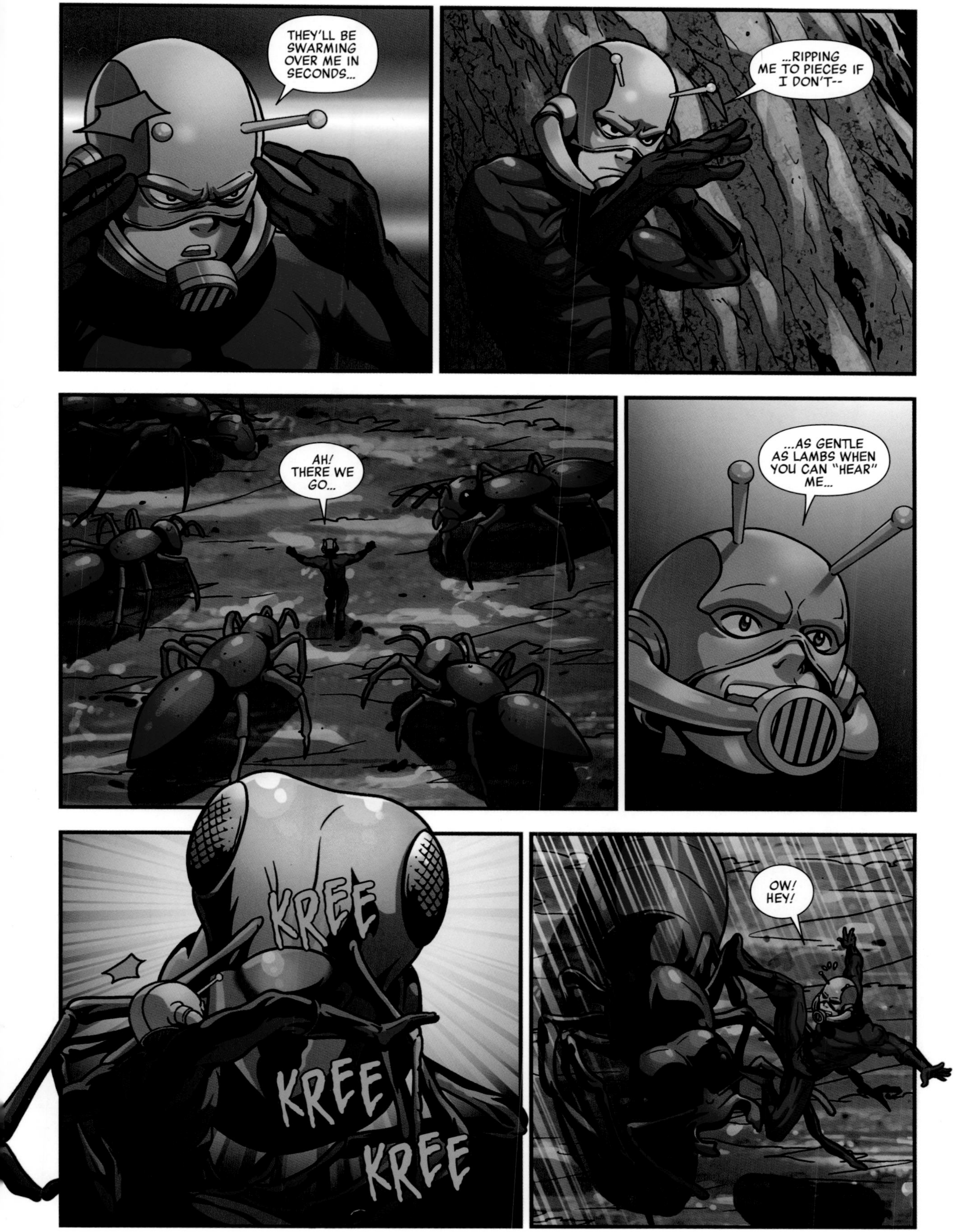
THEY'LL BE SWARMING OVER ME IN SECONDS...
...RIPPING ME TO PIECES IF I DON'T--
AH! THERE WE GO...
...AS GENTLE AS LAMBS WHEN YOU CAN "HEAR" ME...
KREE
KREE
KREE
OW! HEY!

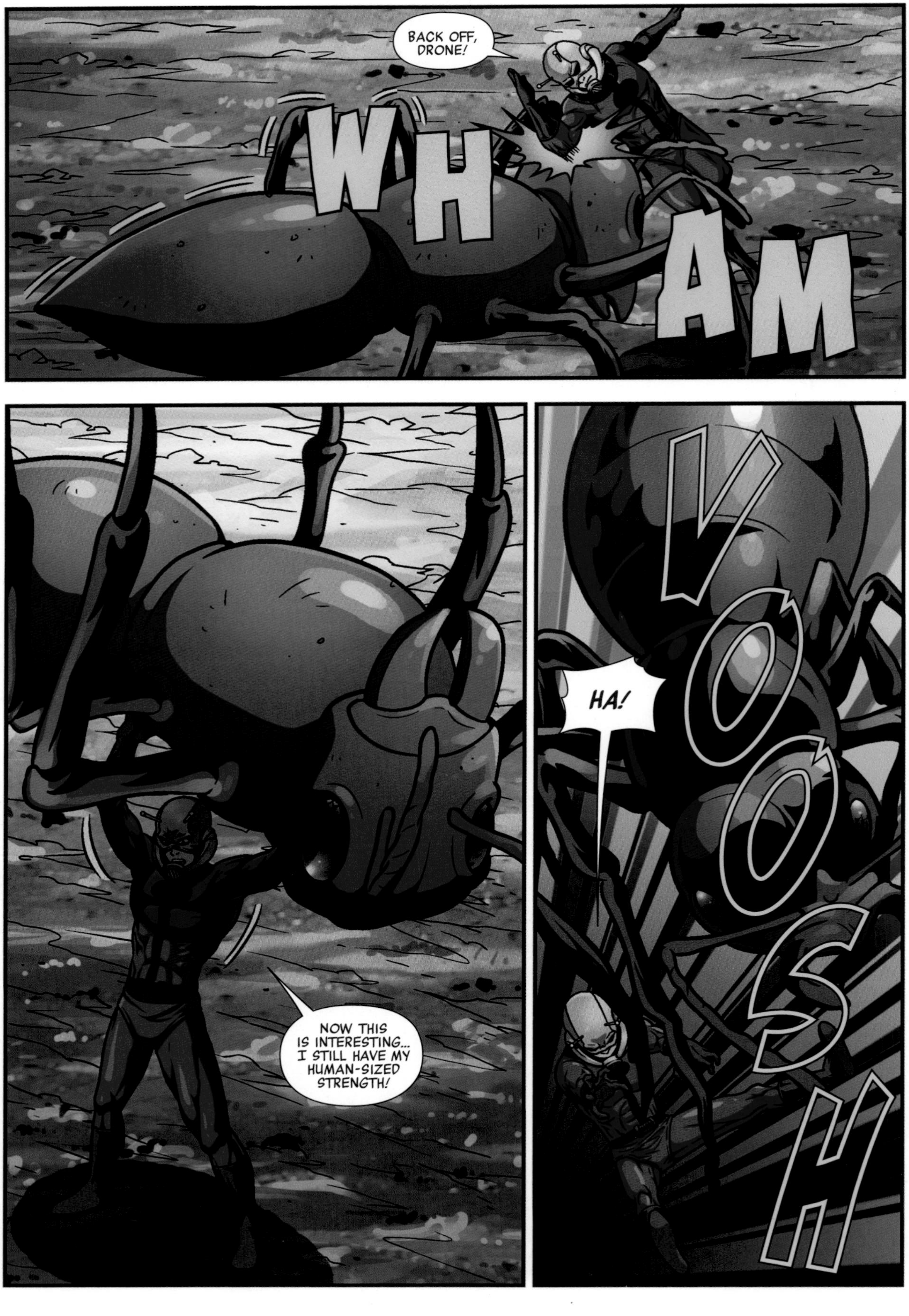
BACK OFF, DRONE!
WHAM
NOW THIS IS INTERESTING... I STILL HAVE MY HUMAN-SIZED STRENGTH!
HA!
VOOOSH

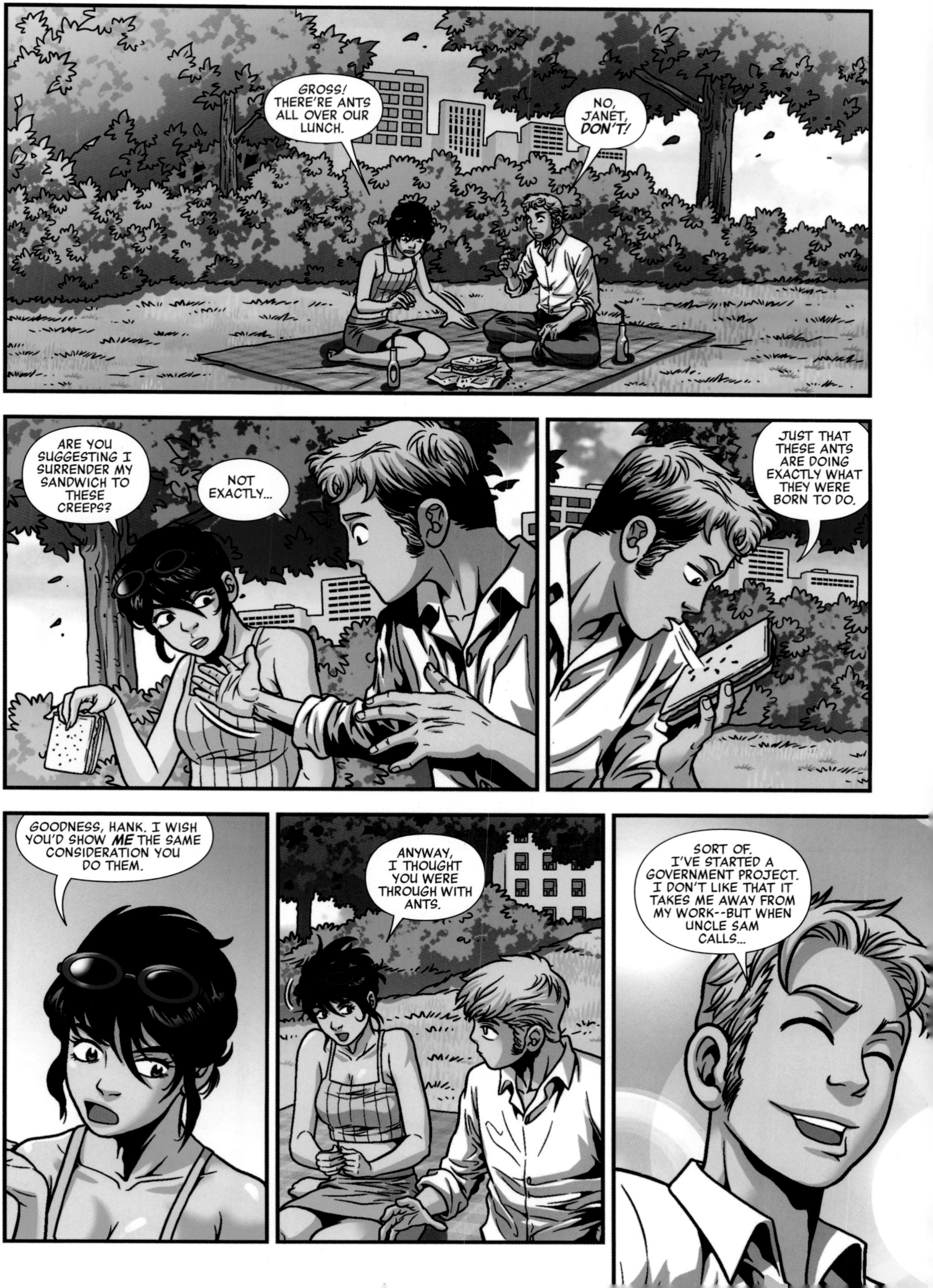
GROSS! THERE'RE ANTS ALL OVER OUR LUNCH.
NO, JANET, DON'T!
ARE YOU SUGGESTING I SURRENDER MY SANDWICH TO THESE CREEPS?
NOT EXACTLY...
JUST THAT THESE ANTS ARE DOING EXACTLY WHAT THEY WERE BORN TO DO.
GOODNESS, HANK. I WISH YOU'D SHOW ME THE SAME CONSIDERATION YOU DO THEM.
ANYWAY, I THOUGHT YOU WERE THROUGH WITH ANTS.
SORT OF. I'VE STARTED A GOVERNMENT PROJECT. I DON'T LIKE THAT IT TAKES ME AWAY FROM MY WORK--BUT WHEN UNCLE SAM CALLS...

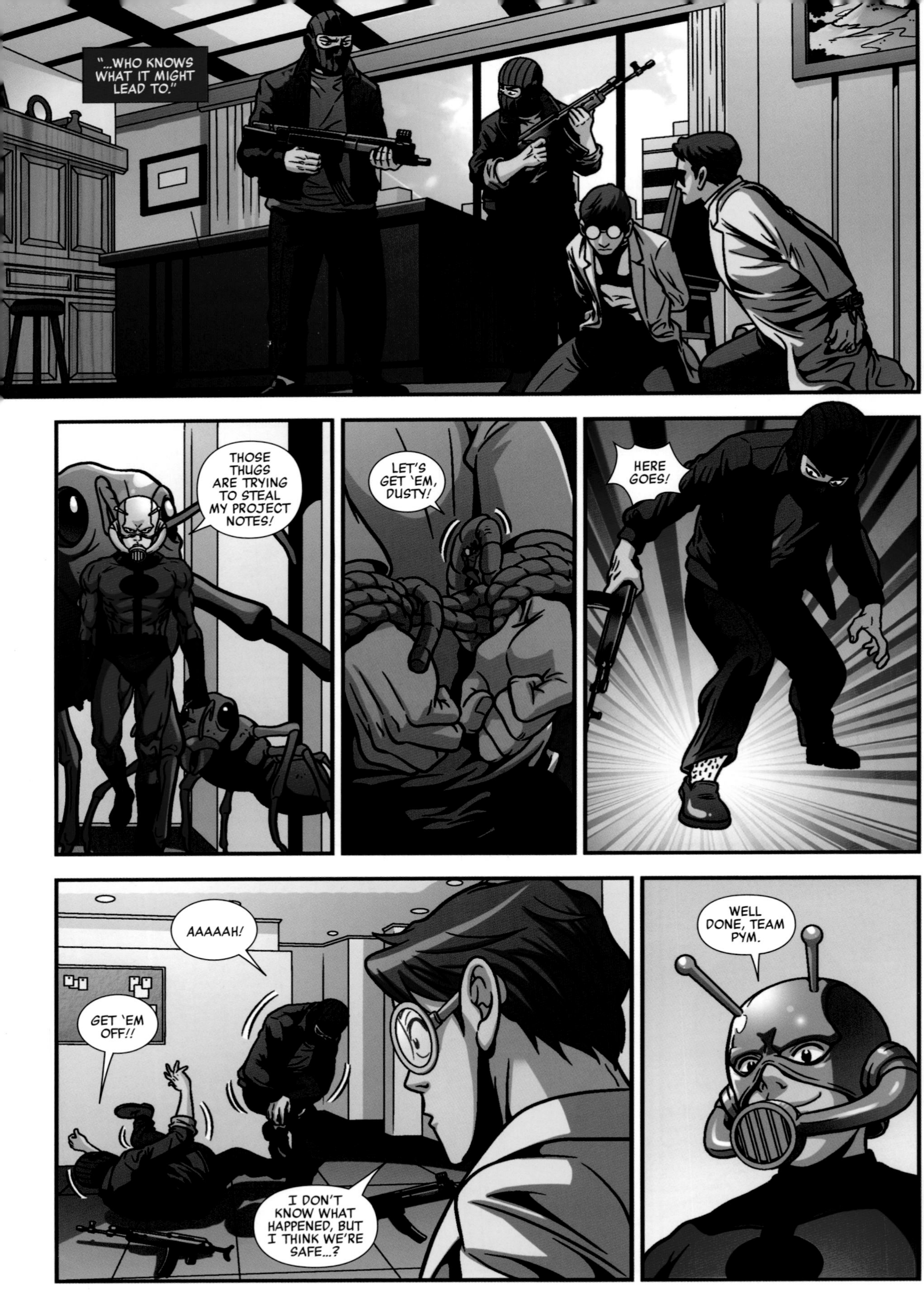
"...WHO KNOWS WHAT IT MIGHT LEAD TO."
THOSE THUGS ARE TRYING TO STEAL MY PROJECT NOTES!
LET'S GET 'EM, DUSTY!
HERE GOES!
AAAAAH!
GET 'EM OFF!!
I DON'T KNOW WHAT HAPPENED, BUT I THINK WE'RE SAFE...?
WELL DONE, TEAM PYM.

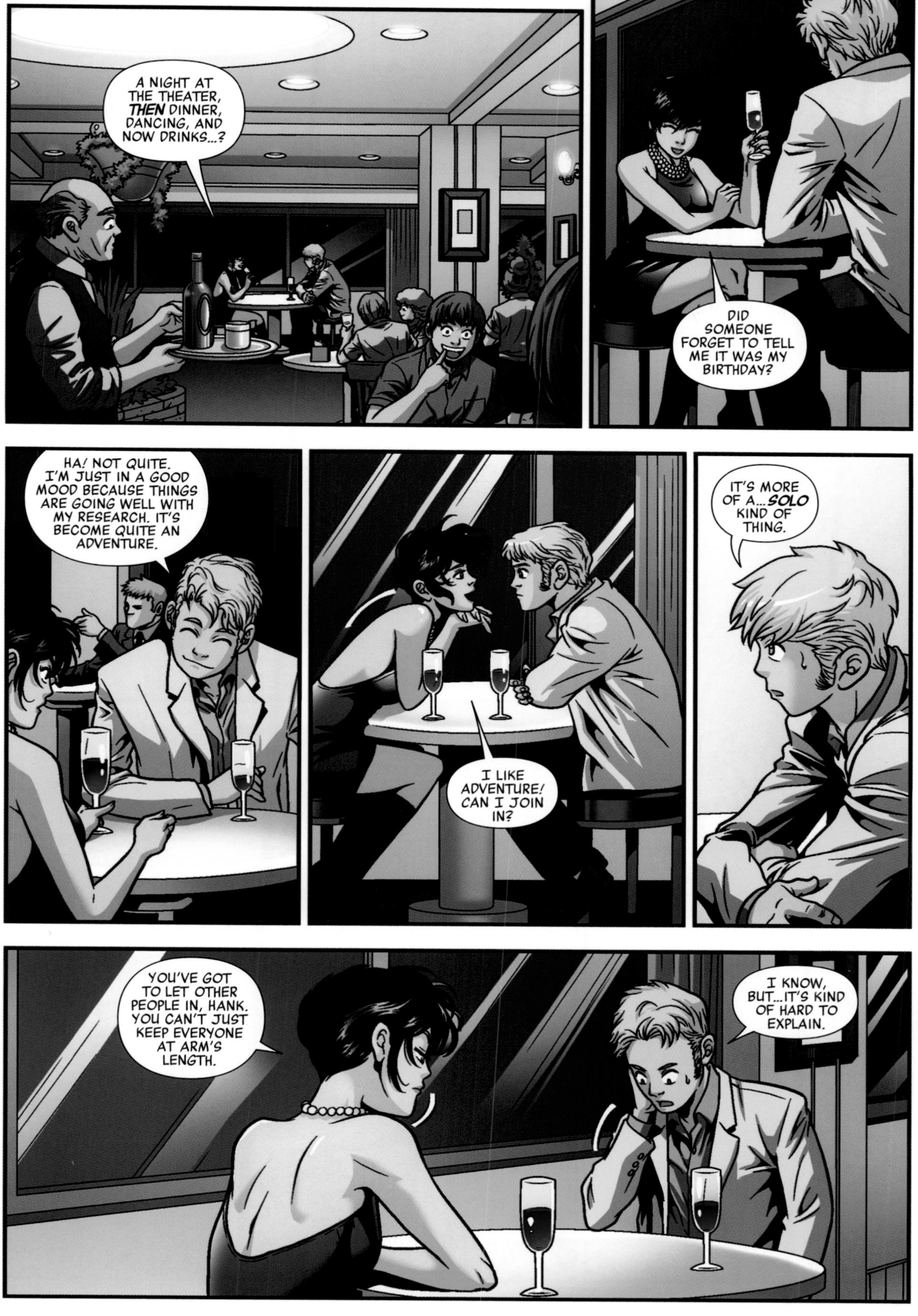
A NIGHT AT THE THEATER, THEN DINNER, DANCING, AND NOW DRINKS...?
DID SOMEONE FORGET TO TELL ME IT WAS MY BIRTHDAY?
HA! NOT QUITE. I'M JUST IN A GOOD MOOD BECAUSE THINGS ARE GOING WELL WITH MY RESEARCH. IT'S BECOME QUITE AN ADVENTURE.
I LIKE ADVENTURE! CAN I JOIN IN?
IT'S MORE OF A...SOLO KIND OF THING.
YOU'VE GOT TO LET OTHER PEOPLE IN, HANK. YOU CAN'T JUST KEEP EVERYONE AT ARM'S LENGTH.
I KNOW, BUT...IT'S KIND OF HARD TO EXPLAIN.

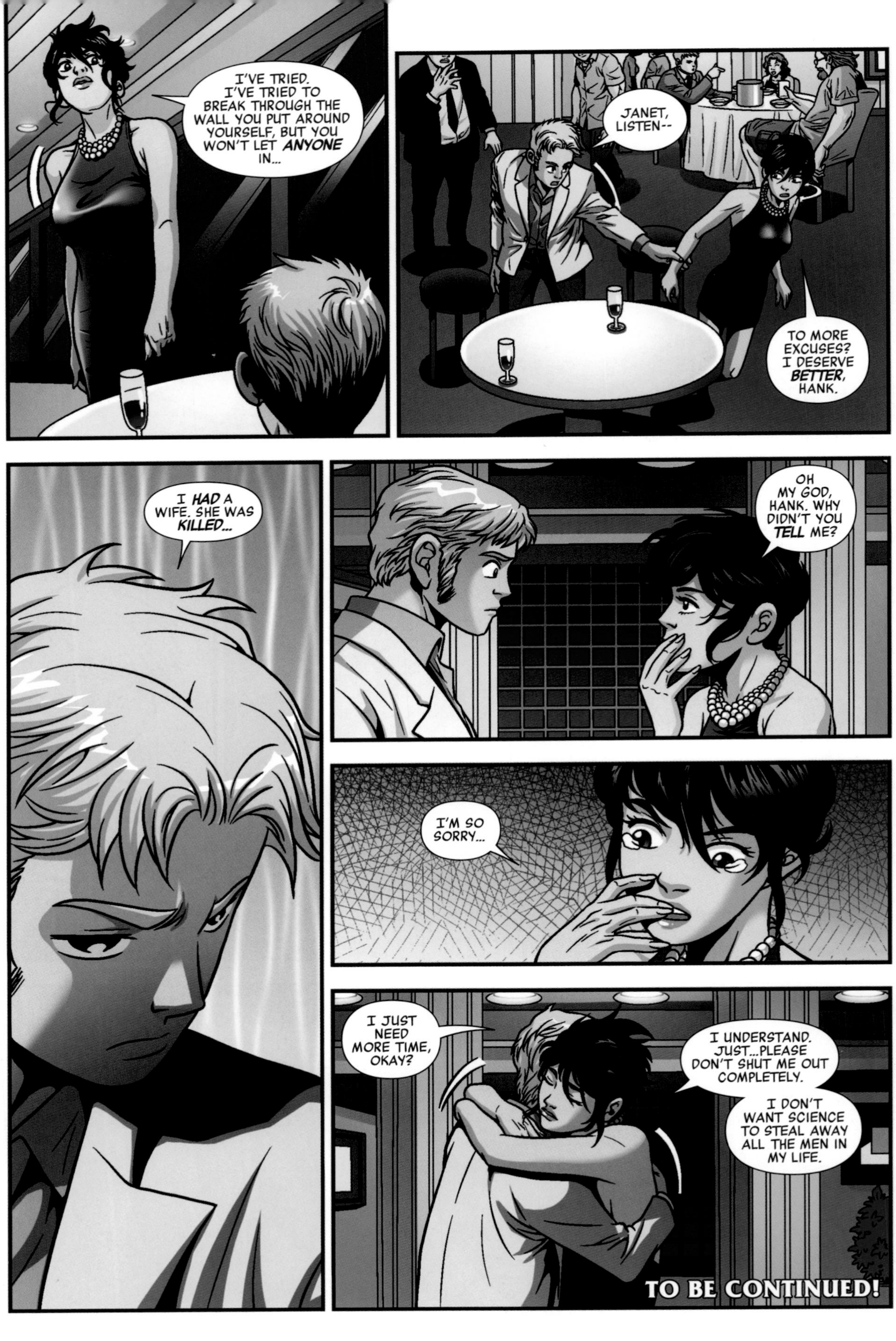

I'VE TRIED. I'VE TRIED TO BREAK THROUGH THE WALL YOU PUT AROUND YOURSELF, BUT YOU WON'T LET ANYONE IN...
JANET, LISTEN--
TO MORE EXCUSES? I DESERVE BETTER, HANK.
I HAD A WIFE. SHE WAS KILLED...
OH MY GOD, HANK. WHY DIDN'T YOU TELL ME?
I'M SO SORRY...
I JUST NEED MORE TIME, OKAY?
I UNDERSTAND. JUST...PLEASE DON'T SHUT ME OUT COMPLETELY.
I DON'T WANT SCIENCE TO STEAL AWAY ALL THE MEN IN MY LIFE.
TO BE CONTINUED!

AVENGERS K
THE ADVENT OF ULTRON

COLLECT THEM ALL!

Set of 6 Hardcover Books ISBN: 978-1-5321-4000-6

AVENGERS K #1
THE ADVENT OF ULTRON
MARVEL

Hardcover Book ISBN
978-1-5321-4001-3

AVENGERS K #2
THE ADVENT OF ULTRON
MARVEL

Hardcover Book ISBN
978-1-5321-4002-0

AVENGERS K #3
THE ADVENT OF ULTRON
MARVEL

Hardcover Book ISBN
978-1-5321-4003-7

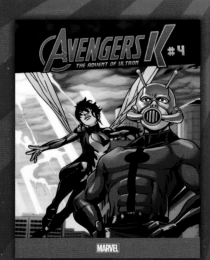

AVENGERS K #4
THE ADVENT OF ULTRON
MARVEL

Hardcover Book ISBN
978-1-5321-4004-4

AVENGERS K #5
THE ADVENT OF ULTRON
MARVEL

Hardcover Book ISBN
978-1-5321-4005-1

AVENGERS K #6
THE ADVENT OF ULTRON
MARVEL

Hardcover Book ISBN
978-1-5321-4006-8